Auntie Claus

and the
Key to Christmas

ELISE PRIMAVERA

SILVER WHISTLE
HARCOURT, INC.

SAN DIEGO   NEW YORK   LONDON · PRINTED IN SINGAPORE

Auntie Claus
NEW YORK   NORTH POLE

Darlings,

The story you are about to be told is absolutely true. It happened one Christmas when my nephew Christopher began to have...doubts, shall we say. The entire family was in a frightful uproar and very cross. Well, we couldn't have that—heavens, no! So, it was up to me to intervene.

Now, hang up your stockings, darlings, and turn this page, for here is where you will find my key to Christmas....

OUNG CHRISTOPHER KRINGLE lived at the Bing Cherry Hotel in New York City, with his parents, the Kringles, and his sister, Sophie. Chris loved going to the Jingle Bell Bell Company, where his father was the president. He spent many happy hours at the Mistle-Toe-to-Nail Salon, which his mother owned. But most of all, Chris loved listening to his great-aunt, Auntie Claus, tell stories about the Kringle family, the North Pole, and Santa.

"Dear boy," she would always say, "when things seem dark and dreary—if times turn sour and bitter—think like a Kringle! You'll soon find your way to all that sparkles and glitters!"

But Chris wasn't so sure. Not anymore.

For he had begun to wonder about his great-aunt. In fact, Chris had begun to wonder about his entire family.

Then, one day, he overheard a pair of out-of-towners, the Spam twins, who were staying at the Bing while on tour promoting their book, *We're Geniuses and Yer Not!* Chris soon learned that Ozzie and Pam were commonly known as the smarty-pants Spams and

had become international sensations....So, how could
he ignore something *they'd* said?

"Hey, Pam," Ozzie sniggered, "it's a week after Halloween
and that lady in the Christmas outfit..."

"...is still in her costume," snickered Pam.

"You'd think she was Santa Claus's sister!" Ozzie snorted.

"Only babies believe in Santa Claus," they chortled.

And so it was that exactly one week after Halloween, Chris repeated what he had heard, and the entire Kringle family was thrown into a tumultuous uproar.

Mrs. Kringle screamed and dropped a full bottle of Mistletoe toenail polish on the carpet.

Mr. Kringle, who was in the process of stringing jingle bells, lost his balance and careened right into the middle of his favorite Christmas tree.

"And you call yourself a Kringle? Shame on you!" said Chris's older sister, Sophie.

To no one's surprise, Chris was immediately summoned to Auntie Claus's suite at the Bing, to penthouse 25C, for tea.

"It has come to my attention," Auntie Claus began, "that there is a nasty rumor going around that some children are saying…well, it's unspeakable! Preposterous! It's completely unacceptable! Marmalade cake, darling?"

Chris squirmed in his seat.

"I have *never* known a Kringle to repeat such things." Auntie Claus paused to stir her tea. "It is time you learned a little family secret. But first there is something you should know about children who start such rumors."

The room suddenly became very quiet. Dark clouds began piling up outside.

"The truth of the matter is that these children eventually become rather… *unattractive* grown-ups. Try some lovely cookies, darling?"

" 'Unattractive?' " Chris asked.

"Yes," said Auntie Claus. "These children become grown-ups who enjoy seeing a birthday cake slip off the edge of a table and go *Splat!* onto the floor. To them, having it rain on the day of a parade is what eating a chocolate éclair is to you. And…they have just formed a club."

"'A club'?" said Chris.

"Yes, darling, *a club*," said Auntie Claus. "It is called the Parade Rainers United National Elite Society, or PRUNES for short."

"Heavens!" Auntie Claus continued. "That *you* of all people would say such a thing…Why, I should think it would rather hurt Santa's feelings."

"Do you know Santa?" Chris asked.

"Why, *of course* I know him—the very idea!" Auntie Claus said.

Sophie rolled her eyes. "Chris is going to be on the B-B-and-G List—again!"

"'B-B-and-G List'?" said Chris.

Auntie Claus sighed. "*B-B-and-G,* darling, is short for Bad-Boys-and-Girls. Anyone on Santa's B-B-and-G List goes without presents for Christmas—so… *unfortunate*."

But Chris was not convinced. "I'll believe it when I see it," he said. "That's my motto!"

"Dear boy, don't you know that all the best things are invisible?" Auntie Claus said. "Sometimes you have to believe *in order* to see. That is *my* motto, that is the key!"

At midnight Auntie Claus left for her annual business trip.

And at midnight Chris was wide-awake. Is there really a B-B-and-G List? he thought. I get presents every year. And to be honest, I'm not all that good.

There was only one way to find out. Chris had made up his mind. "If there really is a B-B-and-G List, my name is going to be on it," he said. "And maybe then I'll get to the bottom of this family secret once and for all!"

The very next day Chris eliminated *please* and *thank you* from his vocabulary. He made rude noises and ate with his mouth open. He whined whenever it looked like someone had something better than he did—and regularly squashed his vegetables in his dinner napkin. For good measure, he started cheating at board games and screaming if he didn't get his own way.

By Christmas Eve, Chris was pretty sure he had covered everything, but he still had doubts. "There is no such thing as the B-B-and-G List!" he said.

"There is, too!" said Sophie.

"I'll believe it when I see it," Chris said.

"What if I told you that I got your name *off* that list last year, because I'm such a nice sister?!" Sophie said.

"You are not!" said Chris.

"Am too!" said Sophie. "And that's not all—Auntie Claus is Santa Claus's older sister!"

"SHE IS NOT!" insisted Chris.

"IS!" shouted Sophie.

"Prove it!" demanded Chris.

"I will," said Sophie. "But you'll have to go on a little trip."

"Fine!" said Chris.

Sophie grabbed her brother's hand and led him up to Auntie Claus's penthouse. *"Sh-h-h-h,"* Sophie said as they tiptoed through the dimly lit apartment to Auntie Claus's private elevator. From inside her jumper, she removed a red-ribbon necklace, at the end of which was a diamond key.

"Look," she whispered. The key glittered in her hand. "If you don't believe me," Sophie said, inserting the key into the lock on the elevator, "then ask Mr. Pudding."

The elevator door slid open.

"I will," said Chris, stepping inside. "Who's Mr. Pudding?"

The door began to close.

"Say that you're the new elf—don't forget!" Sophie said. Suddenly the key sparkled and flashed, illuminating the darkness, and flew from her hand into Chris's just before the door shut.

"What?" said Chris.

The doors closed and the elevator began to move.

"Wait!" Chris screamed.

"Remember, you're the new elf!..." Sophie's voice faded as the elevator rose higher and higher.

"I'm the new elf!" Chris said as the elevator began to pick up speed.

"I'm the n-n-new e-e-elf," he repeated through chattering teeth.

The night was getting colder and colder.

Chris looked around the elevator and was relieved to see a warm jacket, a hat, a pair of mittens, socks, boots, and trousers, all neatly folded in one corner. He quickly put them on and placed the key around his neck. The elevator continued its trip through the starry night.

Thunk! The elevator landed and Chris stepped out.

"I'M THE NEW ELF!" he said loud and clear.

"Hullo, Mr. Pudding here—head elf in charge of vital rules and information!"

"Good," said Chris. "You're just the person I was told to see."

"Oh dear, oh dear. Who did you say you are?"

"The new elf?" said Chris.

"No, you're *not*." Mr. Pudding looked closely at Chris. "*You* are Christopher Kringle. Oh dear, oh dear." He pulled out a little red-and-green book and started to read: "At ten-twelve A.M. (that's Eastern Standard Time) on November eighth through the fourteenth, Christopher Kringle made rude noises, and on those days did not say *please* or *thank you*. Oh dear, let me see . . . vegetable squashing . . . eating with his mouth open . . . We've got quite a bit of insisting on his own way . . . Oh dear, December twentieth—cheating at Candyland?"

Mr. Pudding escorted Chris out of the gates.

"Sorry, but it's a rule—part of arrival procedures: no B-B-and-G's. Meaning, no spoiled brats, no crybabies, and absolutely, positively no one who doesn't *believe*," he whispered. Mr. Pudding closed the gates.

"But, but—," Chris wailed. "I was just trying to get on the B-B-and-G List . . . on purpose!"

"Oh dear, oh dear," said Mr. Pudding. "And no whiners, either!" He locked the gates.

"Mr. Pudding!" Chris called. "You don't understand. It's not my fault— it's Ozzie and Pam's!"

"Ozzie and Pam?" some voices said.

Chris was startled to see a company of snowboys. "You know them?" he said.

"The Spam twins are members in *very* good standing!" they all replied.

"'Members'?" asked Chris.

"They're international sensations," they added.

"Can you help me?" Chris asked. "I've been locked out of Christmas!"

"'Locked out of Christmas'? Come with us. We're on our way to see the High Head. He'll like you!"

Yeah, but will I like *him*, Chris thought, because these snowboys are already starting to get on my nerves.

Yes, we're on the list every year
until we're twenty-one.
But we don't care 'cause being bad
Is just too darn much fun!

And when we're all grown up,
We'll have one great big goal:
to turn your sparkly diamonds
into little lumps of coal.
In short, we love to burst balloons—
our hero's Ebeneezer Scrooge.
And why is that?

Because, because,
BECAUSE
WE'RE . . . "

Down, down, down they marched. It began to drizzle, as the snowboys sang:

"We're spoiled brats, we like to whine—
We're prickly as a porcupine.
We don't believe in you-know-who
Or in reindeer that can fly.
If we don't get our own way,
We'll SCREAM!
We'll BITE!!
WE'LL CRY!!!

"PRUNES!" Chris whispered.

"Welcome!" said the High Head.

There was a flash of lightning. These aren't snowboys, Chris thought, they're PRUNEboys!

Now he could see that not only was the B-B-and-G List real but...his name was the first one on it.

There was a clap of thunder, and it began to rain.

"Lovely!" said the High Head in a booming voice.

"What can I do for you, m'boy?"

"You see, it all started with Ozzie and Pam...," Chris started to explain.

S.J. PRUNE HEADQUARTERS

BB & G's
Christopher Kringle
Oswald Spam

He was beginning to think that maybe those smarty-pants Spams didn't know so much after all.

"Ozzie and Pam *Spam*?" said the head PRUNE. "Fine children—cream of the crop!"

"'Cream of the crop,' Your Royal PRUNEship!" said the PRUNEboys.

"As I was saying, I was locked out of Christmas," Chris continued.

"'Locked out of Christmas'? I'm not sure that even the Spam twins could manage that!" said the head PRUNE.

"They wouldn't even try, O PRUNEiest one!" said the PRUNEboys.

"You're a fine example of a B-B-and-G," said the High Head. "State your name, and like the Spams, you—yes, *you*—can be a lifetime member, guaranteed!"

Member, shmember. I want to go home, Chris thought. He was even beginning to miss Sophie.

"I'm Christopher Kringle," Chris said.

"As in Santa Claus?" said the PRUNE.

"Yes," replied Chris.

The PRUNEboys started to giggle.

"We don't believe in Santa Claus," they snickered.

"I'm Christopher Kringle," Chris said, louder this time, "and I do!"

"Phooey! We don't believe in *you*," jeered the head PRUNE.

Just at that moment, Sophie's key sparkled and flashed in the dreary PRUNElight, and it reminded Chris of something—something he had heard many times but had forgotten: "If times turn sour and bitter—think like a Kringle! You'll soon find your way to all that sparkles and glitters!"

"I'm not a PRUNE, I'm a *Kringle*," Chris said. "And I'm absolutely positive there *is* a Santa Claus…"

A hush fell over the PRUNE headquarters.

"And I don't believe in YOU!" Chris shouted.

Something extraordinary was happening. Were the PRUNEs beginning to shrink? Chris couldn't believe his eyes.

"Now look what you've gone and done!" wailed the head PRUNE.

"Christopher Kringle!" Chris shouted again, as loudly as he could.

The head PRUNE and his PRUNEboys were shriveling up fast now, shriveling up like…well, like prunes.

Then some really strong magic happened. Just as in Auntie Claus's poem, the sour PRUNEs' coal that had been collecting in the PRUNE Hall for ever so long was changing from dark and bitter lumps into diamonds that sparkled and glittered.

Chris found himself whirling around and around through the air at a dizzying speed, in a blur of prune purple into bright Christmas green. He closed his eyes.

When Chris opened his eyes, he saw
he was standing once again outside the gates.
A clock struck midnight
and the gates opened. Santa Claus
circled above and landed.

"HO! HO! HO! Welcome to Christmas!" Santa said.

"Merry Christmas, Santa!" Chris shouted.

Then, from behind the sleigh, out stepped …

"Auntie Claus!" Chris exclaimed.

"My one and only big sister," said Santa. "Couldn't get through a Christmas without her—right, lads?"

"Hooray for Auntie Claus!" everyone cheered.

Turning to Chris, Auntie Claus winked and said, "I knew you had it in you, darling!"

They climbed into the sleigh and headed for the Grand Ballroom.

But there was one thing Chris wondered about. "Santa," he said, "did you happen to get any letters from a couple of twins?"

Before Santa even heard him, Auntie Claus handed Chris two letters. Not surprisingly, they were nearly identical. Just as Chris finished reading them, a gust of wind blew the letters out of his hand. He watched as they vanished into the dark, snowy night.

FROM THE DESK OF
OSWALD SPAM

Deer Santa,
I have bin a very good boy and
I think you shud bring
me lots a prezants but
don't bring any
kos for my sistur
think she dozant
Reel, your
Your Frend,
Ozzie

The sleigh entered the Grand Ballroom, and there were Chris's parents and his sister, Sophie.

"MERRY CHRISTMAS, EVERYONE!" Chris called to his family.

"So, do you believe me now?" Sophie asked her little brother.

Chris took Sophie's diamond key and placed it back around her neck. "Like I always say, think like a Kringle!" Chris said. His cheeks were red and his eyes sparkled.

"He's so much like his uncle," his parents said proudly.

"A real chip off the old block!" said Auntie Claus.

"But shouldn't Chris get a key, too?" Sophie asked.

Chris smiled mysteriously and replied,
"I did get *the key*!"

"Dear boy." Auntie Claus patted his head.
"There's no doubt about it, darling," she whispered
in his ear.

And from that day on there never was...
believe it or not.

My thanks and love to Jack Henderson, great artist,
inspiring teacher, dear friend—E. P.

Library of Congress Cataloging-in-Publication Data
Primavera, Elise.
Auntie Claus and the key to Christmas/Elise Primavera.
p. cm.
"Silver Whistle."
Sequel to: Auntie Claus.

Summary: When Chris expresses doubt about the
existence of Santa Claus, his older sister Sophie reveals
that their aunt is really Santa's sister and helper and then
sends him on a strange journey.
[1. Aunts—Fiction.   2. North Pole—Fiction.   3. Christmas—Fiction.
4. Santa Claus—Fiction.]   I. Title.

PZ7.P93535Aw   2002
[E]—dc21   00-11242
ISBN 0-15-202441-7

H G F E D C B

The illustrations in this book were done in gouache and pastel
on illustration board treated with gesso.
The display lettering was created by Georgia Deaver.
The text type was set in Cloister.
Color separations by Bright Arts Ltd., Hong Kong
Printed and bound by Tien Wah Press, Singapore
Production supervision by Sandra Grebenar and Ginger Boyer
Designed by Judythe Sieck

Auntie Claus
NEW YORK   NORTH POLE

So, as you can see, everything turned out just fine.
Recently I asked Christopher, "Do you remember the year
that you learned about our little family secret?" He chuckled and
said, "Yes, I do, but that year I received the best Christmas gift
ever. To believe is the key—the key to Christmas!"
Yes, the key, darlings—the one that can't be seen. But
then all the best things are invisible.
Love & Merry Kringle, Auntie Claus